Shadow
to the Rescue

Enid Blyton

Illustrated by Rowan Clifford

CARNIVAL

As the summer passed away and autumn came, Shadow the sheepdog grew into a really fine dog. His master, Johnny, was very proud of him and the other sheepdogs on the farm, Rafe, Tinker and Dandy thought twice before they tried to roll him over now. Old Bob did not take much notice of him – but then Bob took very little notice of any other dog!

Shadow spent a great deal of time running over the hills. He wanted to know every inch of them, because Tinker had told him that that was a thing all sheepdogs should know – every foot of their own countryside.

"Then if you are told to take the sheep here, there, or anywhere, you will always know exactly where to go and the shortest way to get there," said Tinker.

Shadow soon knew every field, every valley, every hill, every glen, and every rock. He knew the streams and where they began. He knew the caves in the next hillside and had been in every one of them. He stored all his knowledge away in his sharp doggy mind.

Winter came on. It was cold up in the hills and snow fell early. The old shepherd was expecting new-born lambs before Christmas, and he lived up in his hut with Bob, the mongrel sheepdog. Rafe, Tinker, Dandy, and Shadow went to visit Bob each day.

"Are there any lambs yet?" asked Shadow.

"Two," said Bob. "Come and see them." He took the four dogs to a small pen. Inside lay a big, woolly mother-sheep, and nuzzling by her were two tiny lambs, whose legs looked far too long for their body.

As the winter passed, more and more new-born lambs lay in the folds, or staggered about on unsteady legs. The shepherd was pleased because he had not lost a single lamb. All were strong and healthy, and the farmer was glad.

The weather cleared and the snow melted. The farmer told the dogs to take the sheep to the next hill, where the grass was good. Rafe, Tinker, Bob, Dandy and Shadow set off, with Johnny behind them, eager for the walk.

The sheep were glad to reach the grass on the next hill. It was always good there. The hill was steep and rocky in places, but the turf was sweet and tasty. Soon the whole flock was peacefully grazing there, with the young lambs frisking beside them.

But after two days a queer change came over the sky. It looked heavy and leaden.

"Almost as if it's going to fall down on top of us!" said Johnny to his father. "Is it going to snow again?"

"Yes," said the farmer anxiously. "And it looks as if it will be a heavy fall too. I think we'd better get the sheep back on our own hill in safety. We can pen them there if we need to."

That was a busy afternoon for the five dogs! The great flock of sheep was scattered all over the hills and it needed all the dogs' swiftness and sharpness to get them together. The little lambs ran with their mothers, bleating in fright. The flock was moved off down the hillside to the hill where the shepherd had his hut.

By the time that the dogs had done their work it was snowing heavily. Soon the snow was two or three inches thick. The sky was dark, and it was difficult to work in the half-light.

The shepherd stood by the entrance to the pens. He had put up hurdles for the sheep, and he was counting them as they went inside. He knew every sheep and every lamb.

It was eight o'clock and as dark as pitch before all the sheep and lambs were safely in. The dogs were tired out. All they wanted was to lie by a fire and rest, after a good meal. They looked up at the farmer as he swung his lantern for the shepherd.

"All there, Jim?" he shouted.

"There's a big old ewe missing, and her two small lambs," answered the shepherd. "She was always a wanderer, that sheep. She's maybe taken her lambs over the top of the hill and into the next valley. Well – it's too late to fetch her in now."

"Couldn't one of the dogs go?" said the farmer. "I don't want to lose any sheep, Jim. Let Bob go. He's sharp at finding any of your sheep, no matter where they are."

The shepherd spoke to Bob. The dog got up at once and ran into the night. He knew quite well that he must look for the missing sheep.

Shadow got up too. He wanted to help. He was very tired, but he wanted to find that sheep and the two tiny lambs.

Shadow barked to Bob. But Bob had disappeared into the night. Shadow nosed into the snow and tried to smell Bob's track. The falling snow covered everything, even the smell.

"I'll go after him and see if I can catch him up," thought Shadow. "I know the way to the next hill quite well, even when it is covered with snow!"

And now Shadow was glad that he had explored every inch of the countryside, for even when the hills were covered deep in snow he knew his way!

He did not find Bob. He thought that the sheepdog must have gone another way. Never mind! He would hunt for the lost sheep and lambs by himself. He remembered seeing the old ewe lying down in a sheltered glen the day before. She was a clever one at finding the warmest spots on a cold day. Perhaps she was there!

The dog set off to the glen. He soon came there
and nosed around. But the sheep was not there.
Shadow paused and thought again. Where
would a mother-sheep take her lambs if she
knew that a storm was coming? Sheep were as
clever as dogs in some ways, and they could
smell the weather from afar.

"The caves!" thought Shadow. "I think she
might take her lambs there. She is a silly old
wanderer but she does look after her lambs."

He found his way to the caves. If he had not known every bit of the hillside he could never have reached them, for the hills were now quite different in their blanket of white. The moon came up and the darkness went. Shadow felt a shiver of fright as he saw the world for the first time covered with snow under the pale light of the moon.

He stumbled towards the first cave. Nothing there. He went into the second. Nothing there. He sniffed towards the third – and tails and whiskers, a strong smell of sheep and lambs came to his nose!

"I've found them!" thought Shadow in joy, and he went into the cave. There, huddled at the back, was the big old sheep with her two small lambs. She did not move as the dog came up to her. She was not going to run out into a strange white world!

"You must come with me!" barked Shadow
softly, pushing his nose into her to make her get
up. "Come on! You will be snowed up if you
stay here. You will starve and your young lambs
will die. Come with me before it is too late."

But the old sheep would not move. She was tired and comfortable. Shadow could not make her stir. Outside the snow began to fall again. The dog was almost in despair.

"I wonder if Bob is anywhere near," he thought. "I'll bark and see." So he went to the entrance of the cave, lifted his head and barked loudly over the snowy hillside.

And, not far away, came Bob's answering bark! How Shadow's heart leapt for joy! He barked again – and in a trice old Bob came lumbering over the snow towards the cave.

"I've found the sheep and lambs," said Shadow. "But I can't get the sheep to move."

"I'll soon make her," said Bob. He went into the cave and nosed roughly at the two frightened lambs. They leapt to their feet and ran off to the cave entrance. They stood there and bleated pitifully.

The mother-sheep at once rose to her feet. She would not stir for herself, but for her two little lambs she would do anything!

After that it was easy for the dogs to push her out of the cave and into the snow. The little lambs kept close beside her.

"Shadow, come this way," ordered Bob. "I know where the snow does not lie so thickly."

The five creatures went slowly over the snow. Bob knew the way as well as Shadow, and the sheep followed obediently.

In about an hour's time they came to the pen on the hillside.

"Well, Bob – well Shadow – so you've brought home the wanderers!" cried the shepherd in joy, lifting his lantern high. "Good dogs, both of you. Ah, you're a fine pair, and I'm proud of you!"

"Good work, youngster," said surly Bob, as he said goodnight to Shadow. "Good work."

Shadow was happy as he stumbled down the hill towards the farm. He was tired, so tired that his legs would hardly walk – but he had found the lost sheep, and had won praise from surly old Bob. And what would Johnny say when he heard?

In ten minutes' time the dog lay stretched out before a big fire, his head on Johnny's feet. He slept soundly and in his dreams he hunted for lost sheep. Johnny leaned over and patted him. Shadow opened one eye and sighed joyfully. Could any dog possibly be happier?